Reading Toget

The Tiger and the Jackal

Read it together

This traditional Indian tale tells of a little boy who narrowly escapes being the dinner for a very hungry, untrustworthy tiger. But what upsets the boy most of all is that the tiger broke his promise.

This story is written in a style that helps you to read it aloud in an interesting way. This makes it come alive for children and helps them to understand it better.

Children quickly learn the repeated phrases in the book. Encouraging them to join in with the parts of the story they remember helps build confidence in young readers.

Talking about the story during the reading and afterwards is an important way for children to get to know and make sense of what they read.

Children's questions can take conversations about the story in unexpected directions. This is a good way for them to deepen their understanding of the book and their world.

For the children
of the Primary
Education Centre,
Swansea, V.F.

To Richie,
my big brother.
Big love, Ali.

First published 2001 by Walker Books Ltd
87 Vauxhall Walk, London SE11 5HJ

2 4 6 8 10 9 7 5 3 1

Text © 2001 Vivian French
Illustrations © 2001 Alison Bartlett
Introductory and concluding notes © 2001 CLPE/LB Southwark

This book has been typeset in Providence Sans

Printed in Hong Kong

British Library Cataloguing in Publication Data:
a catalogue record for this book
is available from the British Library

ISBN 0-7445-6878-1

The Tiger and the Jackal

A traditional Indian tale

Retold by **Vivian French**
Illustrated by **Alison Bartlett**

WALKER BOOKS
AND SUBSIDIARIES
LONDON · BOSTON · SYDNEY

There was once a tiger
who was caught in a trap.
"Growl! Growl! Growl!"
said the tiger. "Let me out!"
A boy came running along the road.
Hop! Skip! Jump!

"Let me out," said the tiger,
"and I promise I won't eat you.
Please let me out!"

"Well," said the boy,
"if you promise ... then I will,"
and he opened the trap door.

"Growl! Growl! Growl!" said the tiger.
"Now I shall eat you for my dinner!"
And he pounced on the boy.
"That's not fair!" said the boy.
"You promised!"

"Ho ho!" laughed the tiger. "But I'm a tiger, and
tigers don't keep promises!"
And he opened his mouth
wide wide WIDE.

"Moo! Moo! Moo!"
Just then, a cow came
trudging down the road.

"Cow!" said the boy. "I let the tiger
out of the trap, and now he wants
to eat me for his dinner. He promised
that he wouldn't, so it's not fair, is it?"
"Why not?" said the cow, and she
trudged on.

"See?" said the tiger, and he smiled. "And now I shall eat you for my dinner!"

And he opened his mouth
wide wide WIDE.

Thump! Thump! Thump!
Down the road trundled an elephant.
"Elephant!" said the boy. "I let the tiger
out of the trap, and now he wants
to eat me for his dinner. He promised
that he wouldn't, so it's not fair, is it?"
"Why not?" said the elephant, and he
trundled on.

"See?" said the tiger, and he
smiled even more. "And now
I shall eat you for my dinner!"
And he opened his mouth
wide wide WIDE.

Pitter patter! Pitter patter! Pitter patter!
Down the road pattered a jackal.
"Jackal!" said the boy. "I let the tiger
out of the trap, and now he wants
to eat me for his dinner. He promised
that he wouldn't, so it's not fair, is it?"

"What?" said the jackal, and he sat down.
"What did you let the tiger out of?"
"A trap," said the boy.

The jackal scratched his nose.
"I didn't quite hear you. Say it again."
The tiger's tail began to twitch.
"A trap!" said the boy.
The jackal rubbed his ears.
"Dear me. I'm not hearing
very well today. What did
you say?"

"A trap!" bellowed the tiger.
"I was in a TRAP!"

The jackal put his head on one side.
"But I still don't understand,"
he said.
"GROWL!" roared the
tiger. "You foolish animal!
Look! This is the trap!"

"Oh!" said the jackal. "And where were you?"

"Here!" said the tiger, and he jumped inside the trap.

"Look! Look! LOOK!"

"Aha!" said the jackal. "Now I see."
And he quickly shut the door.

"I think, Mr Tiger, we'll leave you there a little longer, just until you learn to keep your promises!"
And the jackal and the boy ran away together up the road.
Hop! Skip! Jump! Pitter patter!
Pitter patter! Pitter patter!

Read it again

Tell the story
The strong pattern in the story makes it easy to remember. Children can use toy animals to help them tell the story and act it out.

You promised you wouldn't eat me. You're a bad tiger.

I was stuck in the trap so long, I got really hungry.

Masks
With your help, children can make a simple mask of the tiger from the story. They can use it to tell the tiger's side of the story.

Draw a story

Children can draw a picture of one of the characters or their favourite part of the story and use it to tell the story in their own words. They could even make it into a poster for their bedroom wall.

Sort them out

Cats and dogs are traditionally seen as enemies in books and on TV. So in this story the jackal — a wild dog — is keen to help trap the tiger — a big cat. You could collect pictures and toys of cats and dogs, then mix them up and try to sort out which family they belong to.

Reading Together

Reading Together Parents' Handbook
Myra Barrs Sue Ellis

Red Books 2-4 years

Yellow Books 3-5 years

Blue Books 4-6 years

Green Books 5-7 years